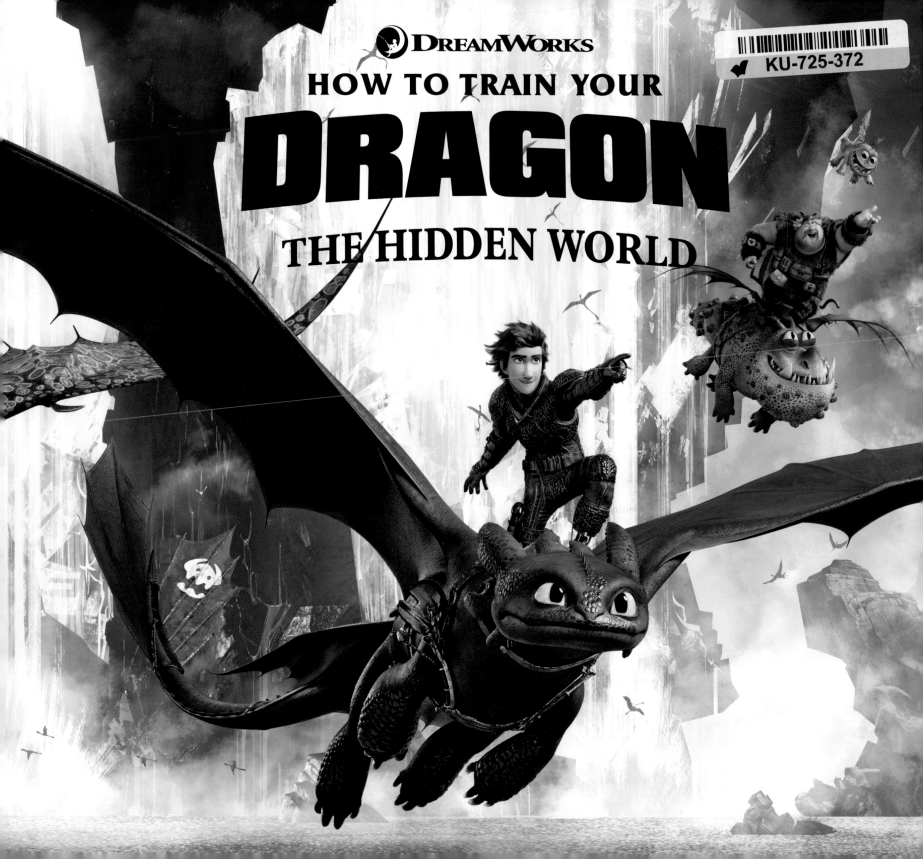

DREAMWORKS

HOW TO TRAIN YOUR
DRAGON
THE HIDDEN WORLD

JOURNEY TO NEW BERK

Home to Vikings for seven generations, the island of Berk is now crowded, noisy and overrun with dragons! In spite of this, Viking chief Hiccup Horrendous Haddock III couldn't be happier – Berk is an island where humans and dragons live peacefully side by side.

But when a ruthless dragon-hunter sets out to capture Hiccup's dragon, Toothless, the last known Night Fury, and the other dragons of Berk, the Vikings are left with no choice... they must disappear, taking their dragons off the map to a place where they can live in peace.

In their search for a legendary Hidden World, the Vikings arrive in a place they call New Berk, a land of sparkling waterfalls, towering peaks and lush valleys – a perfect place for humans and dragons to settle. Read on to discover all about the wildest, most dangerous creatures on Earth, those who tamed them and those who wish to destroy them forever...

FISHLEGS & MEATLUG

HICCUP & TOOTHLESS

SNOTLOUT & HOOKFANG

**RUFFNUT & TUFFNUT
AND BARF & BELCH**

**ASTRID &
STORMFLY**

An unlikely friendship was formed when Hiccup brought down a Night Fury.

After Hiccup trained Toothless, other species of dragons were trained, too.

For centuries, dragons had been the Vikings' deadliest enemies.

TOOTHLESS

One of the cleverest of all dragon species, Toothless is a feared Night Fury. He is thought to be the last of his kind. Jet-black scales cover his whole body and allow him to fly at night without being seen. This loyal dragon is smart, fast and best friends with Hiccup.

FLY A NIGHT FURY

FLY A LIFE-SIZE TOOTHLESS AND HICCUP AROUND YOUR LOCAL PARK!

NIGHT FURY FACTS

🌿 Hiccup created a new left tailfin for Toothless after the dragon's real one was injured in a crash. Now Toothless can fly again but only with his rider, Hiccup, controlling the tailfin with an ingenious saddle Hiccup invented and built.

🌿 Toothless's bravest moment was when he plunged hundreds of metres on his own to save Hiccup from crashing to the ground after the epic battle with the Red Death.

🌿 Toothless is not actually toothless, but he does have retractable teeth that sometimes make him look that way.

🌿 Hiccup's mum, Valka, revealed a row of hidden spikes on Toothless's back that help him to fly even faster.

SPECIAL SPECIES

Toothless has a special ability – echolocation – that is a bit like radar. When his sight is limited, such as in a pitch-black cave, he can emit a sound wave, which bounces off nearby terrain and obstacles, telling Toothless exactly what's around him.

HICCUP

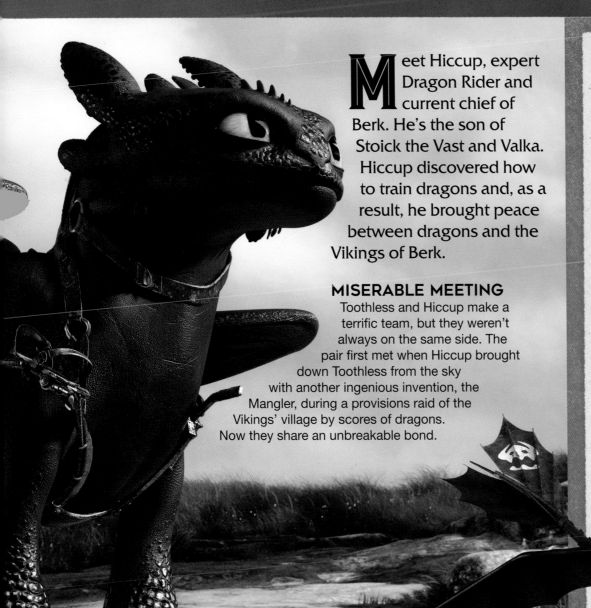

Meet Hiccup, expert Dragon Rider and current chief of Berk. He's the son of Stoick the Vast and Valka. Hiccup discovered how to train dragons and, as a result, he brought peace between dragons and the Vikings of Berk.

MISERABLE MEETING

Toothless and Hiccup make a terrific team, but they weren't always on the same side. The pair first met when Hiccup brought down Toothless from the sky with another ingenious invention, the Mangler, during a provisions raid of the Vikings' village by scores of dragons. Now they share an unbreakable bond.

The Night Fury is the fastest, smartest and rarest of the known dragon species.

 DRAGON STATS

✛ ATTACK	15	⚡ SHOT LIMIT	6
🪶 SPEED	20	☠ VENOM	0
▦ ARMOUR	18	◈ JAW STRENGTH	6
🔥 FIREPOWER	14	▤ STEALTH	18

STORMFLY

TRAIN A TRACKER
TRY YOUR HAND AT HELPING STORMFLY TAKE FLIGHT!

This blue and yellow dragon is as deadly as she is beautiful. She preens and grooms herself like a peacock, and will stop and admire her reflection when passing a mirror-like surface. Don't let her good looks fool you, though! One of the speediest in the skies, Stormfly is hard to beat in a Dragon Race.

PRETTY DEADLY
Deadly Nadder Stormfly may look pretty, but she is deadly in battle. She can shoot poisonous spines from her tail – a powerful secret weapon.

DEADLY NADDER FACTS
- Astrid has taught Stormfly how to fetch like a dog.
- Her favourite treat to eat is chicken.
- Stormfly is part of the Tracker Class of dragons because of her incredible sense of smell and ability to track a human or dragon.
- Deadly Nadders shoot magnesium fire blasts – the hottest of any dragon species.

Fly a life-size **HICCUP** and **TOOTHLESS**!

Try your hand at training **STORMFLY!**

Make **MEATLUG** fly forwards, backwards and hover!

Explore the app to discover more facts and stats about the dragons!

SEVENOAKS

This is a Sevenoaks Book
Text and design Carlton Books Limited 2019

How To Train Your Dragon: The Hidden World © 2019
DreamWorks Animation LLC. All Rights Reserved.

Published in the UK in 2019 by Sevenoaks,
an imprint of Carlton Books Limited
20 Mortimer Street, London W1T 3JW

A catalogue record for this book is
available from the British Library.

ISBN: 978-1-78177-916-3
1 2 3 4 5 6 7 8 9 10
Printed in Dongguan, China

Author: Emily Stead
Executive Editor: Bryony Davies
Design: RockJaw Creative
Design Manager: Emily Clarke
Digital Producer: Will Jones
Production Controller: Nicola Davey

ASTRID

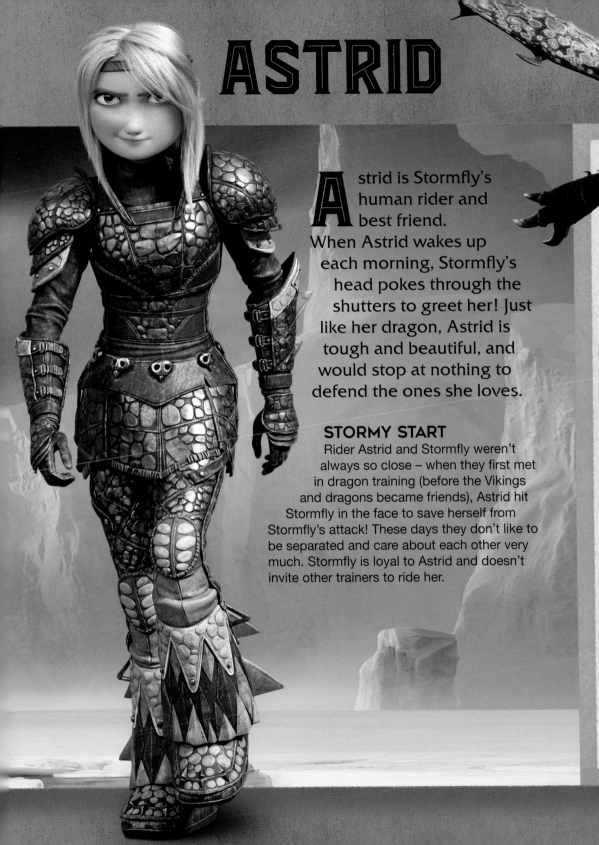

 Astrid is Stormfly's human rider and best friend. When Astrid wakes up each morning, Stormfly's head pokes through the shutters to greet her! Just like her dragon, Astrid is tough and beautiful, and would stop at nothing to defend the ones she loves.

STORMY START

Rider Astrid and Stormfly weren't always so close – when they first met in dragon training (before the Vikings and dragons became friends), Astrid hit Stormfly in the face to save herself from Stormfly's attack! These days they don't like to be separated and care about each other very much. Stormfly is loyal to Astrid and doesn't invite other trainers to ride her.

DRAGON STATS

✚ ATTACK	10	⚡ SHOT LIMIT	6
⛊ SPEED	8	☠ VENOM	16
▦ ARMOUR	16	◆ JAW STRENGTH	5
🔥 FIREPOWER	18	▤ STEALTH	10

Deadly Nadders have blind spots in front of their noses, so it's safest to stand in front of them!

THE DEATHGRIPPERS

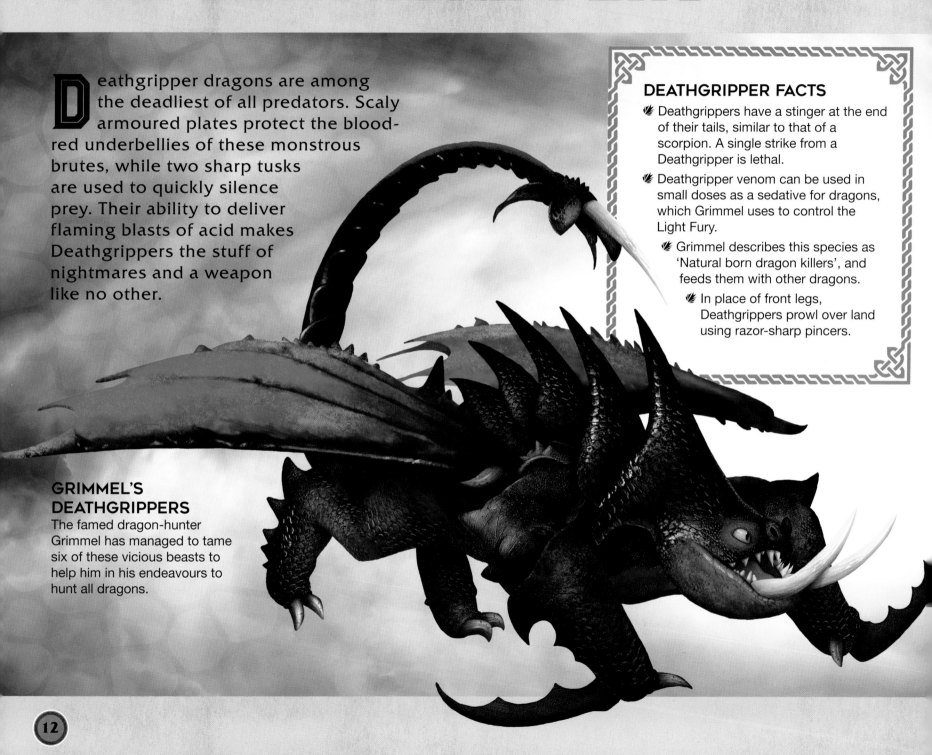

Deathgripper dragons are among the deadliest of all predators. Scaly armoured plates protect the blood-red underbellies of these monstrous brutes, while two sharp tusks are used to quickly silence prey. Their ability to deliver flaming blasts of acid makes Deathgrippers the stuff of nightmares and a weapon like no other.

DEATHGRIPPER FACTS

- Deathgrippers have a stinger at the end of their tails, similar to that of a scorpion. A single strike from a Deathgripper is lethal.

- Deathgripper venom can be used in small doses as a sedative for dragons, which Grimmel uses to control the Light Fury.

- Grimmel describes this species as 'Natural born dragon killers', and feeds them with other dragons.

- In place of front legs, Deathgrippers prowl over land using razor-sharp pincers.

GRIMMEL'S DEATHGRIPPERS

The famed dragon-hunter Grimmel has managed to tame six of these vicious beasts to help him in his endeavours to hunt all dragons.

GRIMMEL

Grimmel is a smart dragon hunter who is outraged at the idea that dragons can live alongside humans. Having believed that he had previously killed all the Night Furies, Grimmel is maddened to learn that the Alpha – Toothless – remains alive and free.

FEARSOME FOE

Grimmel cuts a slender figure and has a shock of white hair. He dresses from head to toe in black, scaly leather and is armed with a deadly crossbow. While Grimmel is ready to strike at any opportunity, he will wait patiently until his target is assured.

IN CONTROL?

Grimmel wants to hunt all dragons, but ultimately he only has the power to subdue them into obedience. He can't control their choices.

DRAGON STATS

⊕ ATTACK	27	⚡ SHOT LIMIT	8
✈ SPEED	12	☠ VENOM	12
☰ ARMOUR	20	◈ JAW STRENGTH	16
🔥 FIREPOWER	12	☰ STEALTH	6

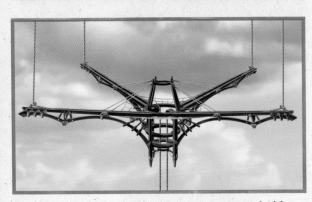

Grimmel travels to his hunts on an austere airship flown by Deathgrippers.

13

THE LIGHT FURY

The Light Fury moves as swiftly as Toothless and, like him, her natural colouring lets her use the skies as camouflage – even during daylight hours. Her white scales allow her to blend perfectly into clouds, sea fog and distant horizons. While she is wary of humans, the Light Fury will wield her plasma blasts to defend any human – or dragon – in need.

OPPOSITES ATTRACT

When Toothless and the Light Fury first meet, the attraction is instant. Toothless is clueless when it comes to flirting! Before long, though, a deep bond grows between the pair – they are as connected as the forces yin and yang.

LIGHT FURY FACTS

- The Light Fury's scales become reflective when she flies through her own plasma blast, making her appear invisible!
- Although the Light Fury prefers the freedom of flying without a rider, and does not trust humans, she eventually forms a connection with Hiccup.
- She is slightly smaller and lighter than her male mate, Toothless.

A TRUE TALENT

Soon after meeting the Light Fury, Toothless discovers his new mate has an incredible talent – she can make herself appear invisible! She blasts a fireball in the sky and then flies directly into it, causing her scales to become reflective of her surroundings. Only a comet-like trail shows that she was ever there.

The Light Fury's wingspan measures almost thirteen metres.

TEACHING TOOTHLESS

The Light Fury tries to teach Toothless how to camouflage himself. It's a tough task!

DRAGON STATS

⊕ ATTACK	15	⚡ SHOT LIMIT	6
🪶 SPEED	20	💀 VENOM	0
▦ ARMOUR	18	💎 JAW STRENGTH	6
🔥 FIREPOWER	14	▤ STEALTH	18

THE HIDDEN WORLD

Hiccup's father, Stoick the Vast, once told his son a legend about a Hidden World, a secret land at the edge of the world, where dragons live totally out of reach of humans and hunters. A vast underground land of beauty, the ancestral home of all dragons. As Berk is no longer a safe haven for dragons, the Vikings must travel in search of the Hidden World if they are to find peace for themselves and the dragons.

The entrance to the Hidden World is a giant caldera (a volcanic crater), a mile wide, beyond the edge of the sea.

Hiccup was just a boy when he was told of the mythical Hidden World.

KING'S ISLAND
The Hidden World is a land of roaring waterfalls and luminous flora, where enormous rocky columns and glowing corals light up the darkness. Deep at its heart is a rocky platform called King's Island.

When Hiccup and Astrid enter the Hidden World on Stormfly, they witness sights that no human has seen before.

The Alpha dragon Toothless and his mate reign majestically over the Hidden World, worshipped by hundreds of dragons of every species – from Armourwings to Typhoomerangs.

MEATLUG

Meatlug is loving and affectionate to her Dragon Rider, Fishlegs. The pair do everything together, from flying to relaxing and hanging out together. Meatlug also accompanies Fishlegs when he researches dragon trivia.

GENTLE DRAGONS

Gronckles may look menacing, but they are a gentle dragon species. They have small, squat bodies and oversized heads. Their fire blast is devastating – a Gronckle chews rocks, then spews them out as balls of molten lava.

FLYING LESSON

MAKE MEATLUG FLY FORWARDS, BACKWARDS AND HOVER!

GRONCKLE FACTS

- Gronckles can be lazy and spend a lot of time napping. They sometimes even fall asleep while flying, often waking up having splashed into the ocean or crashed into the side of a mountain!

- Gronckles are the only dragons known to fly forwards, backwards and sideways – and they can even hover thanks to their compact, fast-fluttering wings.

- When Gronckles ingest more than one rock at a time, they will occasionally spit out a brand-new substance in lava form.

- Baby Gronckles don't hatch from eggs like other dragon species; they explode out of their shells!

FISHLEGS

 Meatlug's lovable rider Fishlegs adores all dragon species, and keeps detailed records of their strengths and weaknesses. Unlike other Vikings, Fishlegs isn't a rule-breaker – he prefers to play it safe. But he will always do whatever it takes to protect Meatlug and his friends.

DRAGON STATS

⊕ ATTACK	8		⚡ SHOT LIMIT	6
⪢ SPEED	4		☠ VENOM	0
⊞ ARMOUR	20		◈ JAW STRENGTH	8
🔥 FIREPOWER	14		▤ STEALTH	5

Meatlug is sweet and affectionate – just like her rider, Fishlegs!

PERFECT PAIRING
Fishlegs and Meatlug really are the perfect pair. Meatlug likes to lick Fishlegs's feet before they go to sleep and Fishlegs often makes up songs about Meatlug and calls her 'Princess Meatlug'.

HOOKFANG

A powerful fire-breather, the Monstrous Nightmare Hookfang is huge. While most dragons obey their riders, disobedient Hookfang often chooses to do the opposite of what Snotlout tells him! Despite Hookfang not listening to Snotlout, they are both warriors at heart.

MONSTROUS NIGHTMARE FACTS

- This dragon species truly is the stuff of nightmares! It's enormous, stubborn and does exactly as it likes.
- Monstrous Nightmares can not only breathe fire, but also emit kerosene from their pores to set their skin alight. No damage is done to the dragon, but it's a frightening sight for its enemy.
- Hookfang has an incredible wingspan of more than 20 metres.
- Hookfang's horns lack extra antlers, which helps Snotlout to tell him apart from other Monstrous Nightmares.

NIGHTMARE IN FLIGHT

DARE YOU TAKE CONTROL OF THE FIERY HOOKFANG?

SNOTLOUT

Bullheaded Snotlout is Hookfang's rider. Snotlout's main gift is his strength – he is often seen carrying sheep above his head – which goes a little way to make up for his brutish behaviour. Stubborn and arrogant, Snotlout is not unlike his dragon. Although Hookfang almost never follows Snotlout's commands, the pair do care for one another.

DRAGON STATS

⊕ ATTACK	15	⚡ SHOT LIMIT	10
🦅 SPEED	16	☠ VENOM	0
▦ ARMOUR	12	💎 JAW STRENGTH	6
🔥 FIREPOWER	15	▤ STEALTH	9

When Snotlout wields his hammer, he and Hookfang make a fearsome duo!

DRAGON TRAINING

At first, Snotlout was wary of dragons. He would rather strike first and ask questions later. But with Hiccup's help, Snotlout managed to make friends with Hookfang and become his rider. Now they make a tremendous team, either in combat or in competition with the other Dragon Riders.

BARF & BELCH

Barf & Belch belong to the Hideous Zippleback species, an unusual and dangerous type of dragon. Just like the twins that ride them, Barf & Belch spend more time bickering than working together, proving that two heads are not always better than one. They are strong and agile, but can get their necks in a tangle at times.

FLAMING GAS!

WATCH BARF & BELCH IGNITE A BALL OF GAS BEFORE YOUR VERY EYES!

HIDEOUS ZIPPLEBACK FACTS

- This Mystery Class dragon has two long, spiked serpentine necks. The spikes can lock together and create the illusion of one neck.

- Even without Belch's spark, Barf's gas is a thick green substance that can provide adequate cover for evading capture or attack.

- Instead of breathing fire, one head breathes a thick green gas, then the other head ignites it – an explosive combination!

RUFFNUT & TUFFNUT

Twins Ruffnut & Tuffnut are a danger-loving duo. They share a passion for taking risks - no challenge is too deadly for Ruff & Tuff! Sister Ruff has a snarky manner and is quite the tomboy, while her brother Tuff is fearless and daring.

DRAGON STATS

⊕ ATTACK	12	⚡ SHOT LIMIT	6
🪶 SPEED	10	💀 VENOM	0
Ⓜ ARMOUR	10	💎 JAW STRENGTH	6 (3X2)
🔥 FIREPOWER	14	▤ STEALTH	22 (11X2)

TWIN RIDERS
When Ruffnut & Tuffnut took charge of Barf & Belch, they used to shout instructions to their dragons at the same time. The result was chaos! These days the riders and dragons work as a team (most of the time).

Barf & Belch spend a lot of their time bickering, but occasionally they do get along.

SKULLCRUSHER

Skullcrusher was the first of the Rumblehorn species of dragons to be discovered by the Vikings. These Tracker Class dragons can sniff out targets from the faintest of scents – they are the dragon version of a bloodhound! Skullcrusher tracked down Hiccup in Valka's nest with Hiccup's lost helmet the only clue.

HEADSTRONG HERO
Skullcrusher once tried to warn the Dragon Riders that a tidal wave was on its way, but the only Viking who believed him was Stoick. With Skullcrusher's help, Stoick and the riders were able to save the outpost, just in time.

DRAGON STATS

ATTACK	11	SHOT LIMIT	4
SPEED	7	VENOM	0
ARMOUR	12	JAW STRENGTH	5
FIREPOWER	22	STEALTH	6

RUMBLEHORN FACTS
- The rough Rumblehorn has a rhino-like head, which it uses as a battering ram.
- A Rumblehorn's secret weapon is its ability to launch long-range fiery missile-like blasts.
- Stoick named his Rumblehorn 'Skullcrusher', as they both have heads as hard as iron.
- Skullcrusher became Stoick's dragon after he released Thornado to raise some infant Thunderdrums.

STOICK, ERET & VALKA

Stoick the Vast was chieftain of Berk at a time when Vikings and dragons were enemies. After Hiccup brought peace to the island, Stoick's job became much easier. Stoick and Hiccup hardly ever saw eye to eye, but in the end, the chief could not have been prouder of his son.

LEGEND
Stoick died in an accident when Toothless was tricked into attacking him. A mountain of a man, Stoick will remain in Viking legend forever.

VALKA
Valka is Hiccup's long lost mother and wife of Stoick. She lived among dragons for nearly 20 years, where she discovered many of their secrets and learned their ways. Valka has always fought for dragons' freedom and her fearless companion is a Stormcutter called Cloudjumper.

ERET
Eret, Son of Eret, is both cocky and kind-hearted. He became Skullcrusher's rider following the death of Stoick. Once a dragon trapper who used to work for Drago Bludvist, Eret is now loyal to the Vikings, and is Hiccup's right-hand man.

GRUMP

Grump belongs to a breed of Boulder Class dragons known as Hotburple. Its body is covered in grey and copper-coloured scales, and its ears and teeth look similar to a Gronckle. While Gronckles eat boulders to create their fiery blasts, Hotburples shoot flaming chunks of lava.

HOTBURPLE FACTS

- Hotburples eat a diet of scraps of iron ore, which they use to make slugs of molten lava.
- Like Gronckles, Hotburples are lazy layabouts. Their snores are obnoxiously loud!
- The Hotburple's wingspan is much bigger than a Gronckle's, and the bludgeon on its tail is rounder and bulbous.
- Of all the dragon species, the Hotburple is the only one strong enough to bite through dragon-proof bars.

LAZY BUT LOYAL

Grump is extremely lazy and prone to falling asleep anywhere, from his rider Gobber's stall to mid-flight! Grump is devoted to Gobber and would do anything to help him.

GOBBER

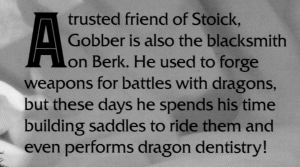

A trusted friend of Stoick, Gobber is also the blacksmith on Berk. He used to forge weapons for battles with dragons, but these days he spends his time building saddles to ride them and even performs dragon dentistry!

FAITHFUL SERVANT

Steadfast Gobber is incredibly loyal and is always willing to help his Viking clan. He is a great mentor with a huge heart and would do anything for anyone – he just doesn't want anyone to know it!

DRAGON STATS

⊕ ATTACK	8	⚡ SHOT LIMIT	6
🗡 SPEED	4	☠ VENOM	0
▥ ARMOUR	20	💎 JAW STRENGTH	8
🔥 FIREPOWER	14	▤ STEALTH	5

Gobber is known on Berk for his bravery, having lost a hand and a leg to a Monstrous Nightmare.

Gobber and Stoick were the best of friends and always supported each other.

MEET MORE DRAGONS

Living side by side with dragons has taught Hiccup and the Vikings far more about these dynamic dragons than is revealed in Bork the Bold's *Book of Dragons*. Every dragon is different, but equally fascinating. These four dragons are just a few of the amazing species known to the Dragon Riders.

 ## THUNDERDRUM

This sea dragon doesn't need to breathe fire to terrify – the sonic boom it creates in its enormous mouth is so strong it can wipe out an opponent from close range. The dragon likes to skim the surface of the ocean, ready to dive beneath the waves and swallow up a whole school of fish in one swoop. Stoick once rode a Thunderdrum called Thornado.

✪ ATTACK	12	⚡ SHOT LIMIT	6
🪶 SPEED	14	💀 VENOM	0
🟫 ARMOUR	10	💎 JAW STRENGTH	7
🔥 FIREPOWER	16	▦ STEALTH	8

 ## STORMCUTTER

Valka's dragon is a sturdy Stormcutter called Cloudjumper, with fins that sprout from his face and tail. A second set of wings are revealed to allow the dragon to fly in an X formation and make tight turns. The sharp, hooked talons on its wings are nimble enough to pick the lock of a dragon trap, yet strong enough to tear an enemy to shreds.

✪ ATTACK	10	⚡ SHOT LIMIT	8
🪶 SPEED	8	💀 VENOM	0
🟫 ARMOUR	4	💎 JAW STRENGTH	5
🔥 FIREPOWER	12	▦ STEALTH	13

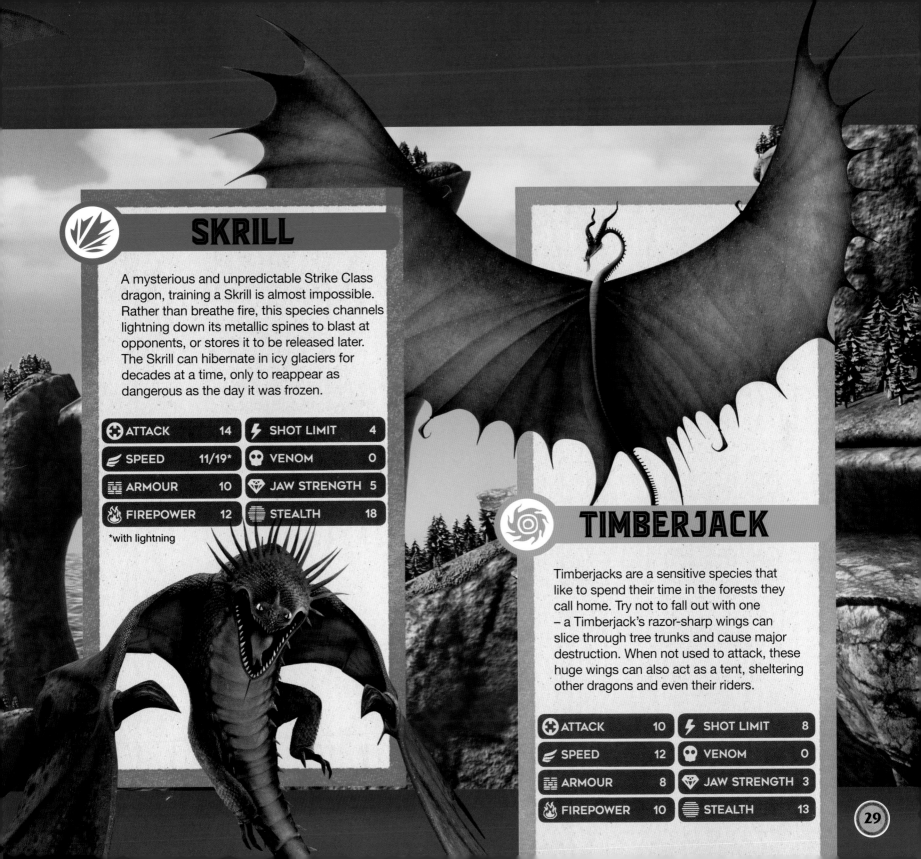

SKRILL

A mysterious and unpredictable Strike Class dragon, training a Skrill is almost impossible. Rather than breathe fire, this species channels lightning down its metallic spines to blast at opponents, or stores it to be released later. The Skrill can hibernate in icy glaciers for decades at a time, only to reappear as dangerous as the day it was frozen.

⊕ ATTACK	14	⚡ SHOT LIMIT	4
🪶 SPEED	11/19*	💀 VENOM	0
▦ ARMOUR	10	💎 JAW STRENGTH	5
🔥 FIREPOWER	12	▦ STEALTH	18

*with lightning

TIMBERJACK

Timberjacks are a sensitive species that like to spend their time in the forests they call home. Try not to fall out with one – a Timberjack's razor-sharp wings can slice through tree trunks and cause major destruction. When not used to attack, these huge wings can also act as a tent, sheltering other dragons and even their riders.

⊕ ATTACK	10	⚡ SHOT LIMIT	8
🪶 SPEED	12	💀 VENOM	0
▦ ARMOUR	8	💎 JAW STRENGTH	3
🔥 FIREPOWER	10	▦ STEALTH	13

TRAINER QUIZ

How would you fare in the field as a Dragon Rider? Are you a top trainer, like Hiccup and Valka, or more of a dragon dunce? Try these tricky trainer quiz questions, then work out your score.

1. Which dragon can deliver a deafening sonic boom blast?

2. Which dragon became Hiccup's hero when he saved him from the Red Death?

3. Which dragon has a blind spot in front of its nose?

4. Name the two species whose attack method is to chew rocks and release them as molten lava.

5. Which baby dragon species explodes out of its shell at birth?

6. Which rare dragon can make itself appear invisible?

7. Which dragon type does this symbol represent?

8. Look closely to discover the only dragon in this book that has no legs.

9. Grimmel uses which species' venom to control dragons?

10. Look back through the book to find the speediest dragon.

11. Which dragon has fins that sprout from its face and tail?

12. Which dragon species does not breathe fire?

Answers

1. Thunderdrum, 2. Toothless, 3. Deadly Nadder, 4. Gronckle and Hotburple, 5. Gronckle, 6. Light Fury, 7. Strike Class, 8. Timberjack, 9. Deathgripper, 10. Toothless, 11. Stormcutter, 12. Skrill.